“GALACTIC DIPLOMACY: A JOURNEY THROUGH THE STARS”

MANEET NAGAMALLA

Made with ♥ on the Notion Press Platform
www.notionpress.com

Contents

CHAPTER I

"First Contact"

Kara sat in the cramped shuttle, her stomach churning with a mix of excitement and nerves. She had been dreaming of this moment for years, ever since she had first set her sights on becoming a diplomat for the United Nations of Earth. And now, finally, she was about to make first contact with an alien species.

The shuttle was en route to a small planet on the outskirts of the galaxy, where a delegation from an alien species had requested a meeting with Earth representatives. It was a historic moment, one that could change the course of human history forever.

Kara had been chosen to lead the negotiations on behalf of humanity, a task that was both exhilarating and terrifying. She had spent months preparing for this moment, studying the alien culture and language as best she could with the limited information available. But she knew that no amount of preparation could truly prepare her for the reality of making contact with an entirely different species.

As the shuttle descended towards the planet's surface, Kara's heart raced with anticipation. She could see the alien delegation waiting for them on a nearby landing pad, their sleek ships hovering above. Kara took a deep breath, trying to steady her nerves, before leading her team out of the shuttle and towards the aliens.

The first meeting was awkward and tense, with both sides struggling to communicate due to the language and cultural barriers. Kara and her team had brought along translators, but even with their help, it was clear that communication would be a major hurdle to overcome in the negotiations.

Despite the challenges, Kara couldn't help but feel a sense of wonder and excitement as she looked at the aliens. They were nothing like anything she had ever seen before, with strange, shimmering skin and elongated limbs. Their language sounded like a series of clicks and whistles to her ears, and she struggled to make sense of their gestures and expressions.

As the first day of negotiations drew to a close, Kara and her team returned to their temporary living quarters to debrief and rest. Kara sat alone in her room, her mind racing with thoughts and questions about the aliens and the negotiations to come. She knew that the road ahead would be difficult and uncertain, but she was determined to do everything in her power to make the negotiations a success.

As she lay down to sleep, Kara couldn't help but wonder what the future held for humanity and this newfound alliance with an alien species. Would it lead to peace and prosperity, or would it ultimately lead to conflict and chaos? Only time would tell, but for now, Kara was simply grateful for the opportunity to be a part of this historic moment in human history.

CHAPTER II

"Cultural Differences"

Kara woke up early the next morning, eager to start the second day of negotiations with the alien delegation. Despite the fatigue from the long journey and the challenges of the previous day's discussions, she felt energized by the possibilities of what they might accomplish.

As she made her way to the meeting room, Kara's mind raced with thoughts of the cultural differences that were becoming more apparent with each passing moment. She had studied the alien culture extensively in the months leading up to the meeting, but now that she was face-to-face with them, it was clear that there were still many things she did not understand.

The alien delegation appeared to be equally fascinated by the humans, and there were several moments of awkward silence as both sides tried to navigate the language and cultural barriers. Kara found herself relying more on her intuition and instincts than on her training, hoping that she could read the nuances of the alien delegation's expressions and gestures to better understand their thoughts and emotions.

One major cultural difference that quickly became apparent was the way that the aliens viewed time. They had a much longer lifespan than humans and appeared to be in no hurry to reach any particular outcome. Kara found herself growing impatient with their slow pace, but she knew that rushing them would only cause offense.

Another major difference was the way that the aliens approached communication. They were much more indirect in their language, often speaking in metaphors or using roundabout ways of expressing themselves. This led to several misunderstandings and moments of confusion during the negotiations, and Kara knew that they would need to find a way to bridge this gap if they were going to make progress.

Despite these challenges, Kara remained hopeful that they could find common ground. She was particularly heartened by the way that the aliens seemed to value diplomacy and peaceful conflict resolution. It was clear that they did not want to be seen as aggressors or conquerors, and Kara hoped that this shared value could be a foundation for building trust and understanding.

As the second day of negotiations drew to a close, Kara found herself mentally and emotionally exhausted. She retreated to her quarters, hoping to find some time to rest and recharge before the next day's discussions. As she lay in bed, she couldn't help but wonder what other cultural differences they would encounter, and how they would overcome them to achieve their goals. It was a daunting task, but Kara was determined to see it through to the end.

CHAPTER III

"Trust Issues"

The third day of negotiations began with a sense of tension in the air. Kara sensed that something was off, but she couldn't quite put her finger on it. As she entered the meeting room, she saw that the alien delegation was already there, waiting for her and her team.

Kara tried to put on a brave face and project confidence, but she felt a knot forming in her stomach. She wondered if something had gone wrong, if the aliens had changed their minds about cooperating with the humans, or if there was some other problem that she had not anticipated.

The negotiations started out civilly enough, with both sides presenting their proposals and discussing potential areas of agreement. But as the discussions continued, Kara noticed that the aliens seemed to be growing more guarded and defensive.

It became clear that the trust that had been built up over the past two days was beginning to erode. The aliens seemed to be suspicious of the humans' motives, and Kara could sense that they were becoming increasingly reluctant to share information or make concessions.

Kara knew that she needed to find a way to restore the trust that had been lost. She tried to think of ways to reassure the aliens, to show them that the humans were sincere in their desire for a mutually beneficial partnership. But it was difficult to know where to start.

One of the alien delegates, a tall, thin creature with a serious expression, spoke up. "We are concerned that the humans may not have our best interests at heart," he said.

"We are a vulnerable species, and we cannot afford to be taken advantage of."

Kara took a deep breath and tried to remain calm. "I understand your concerns," she said. "But I assure you that the humans are committed to finding a solution that is fair and equitable for both of our species. We have no interest in exploiting or harming you in any way."

The alien delegate nodded, but Kara could tell that he was not entirely convinced. She knew that words alone were not enough to rebuild the trust that had been lost. She needed to find a way to demonstrate the humans' good intentions.

As the negotiations continued, Kara began to think of ways to do just that. She suggested that the humans offer a show of good faith, perhaps by sharing some of their advanced technologies or offering to collaborate on a joint scientific project.

The idea was met with cautious approval from the aliens, and Kara could see the beginnings of a thaw in the icy atmosphere that had settled over the negotiations. By the end of the day, she felt cautiously optimistic that they could find a way to move forward.

As Kara left the meeting room, she knew that there was still a long road ahead. The trust issues that had arisen could not be solved overnight, and there were sure to be many more challenges and obstacles to come. But she was determined to find a way to bridge the gap between the humans and the aliens, and to build a partnership that would benefit both of their species for generations to come.

CHAPTER IV

"The Discovery"

As Kara walked through the dimly lit corridors of the research facility, her mind was still focused on the tense negotiations from the previous day. She knew that restoring trust with the alien delegation would be a long and difficult process, and she was eager to find a way to demonstrate the humans' good intentions.

But as she entered the lab, she noticed something strange. The normally bustling room was quiet, and the scientists who were usually bustling about their workstations were huddled around a large screen at the center of the room.

Kara made her way over to the group and looked at the screen. At first, she wasn't sure what she was looking at. It was a series of complex equations and diagrams, and it was clear that whatever the scientists had discovered, it was of great importance.

One of the lead scientists turned to her, a look of amazement on his face. "Kara, you're not going to believe this," he said. "We've made a breakthrough in our research on the alien technology."

Kara felt a surge of excitement. "What have you found?" she asked eagerly.

The scientist pulled up a series of images on the screen, showing a small device that looked like a sleek silver bracelet. "This is a communication device that we believe was used by the aliens to communicate with each other," he said. "But that's not the most interesting part. When we reverse engineered the technology, we discovered that it contains a sophisticated form of artificial intelligence."

Kara's eyes widened in surprise. "What do you mean?" she asked.

The scientist explained that the device was able to learn from its surroundings and adapt to new situations, and that it was far more advanced than anything the humans had ever developed. He also explained that it had the ability to translate languages, which would be a game-changer for the negotiations.

Kara could barely contain her excitement. She knew that this discovery had the potential to revolutionize the way that humans and aliens communicated with each other. It was a breakthrough that could make the negotiations much smoother and more productive, and it would help to restore the trust that had been lost.

But as she looked at the device on the screen, she couldn't help but wonder what else the aliens were capable of. If this small communication device was so advanced, what other incredible technologies were they hiding? And what other secrets were waiting to be discovered?

As the scientists continued to work on the device, Kara couldn't help but feel a sense of awe and wonder. She knew that they were standing on the brink of a new era of human-alien relations, and that there was no telling what other incredible discoveries were waiting to be made. She was eager to see what the future held, and she knew that she and her team were at the forefront of a truly groundbreaking moment in human history.

CHAPTER V

"The Saboteur"

Kara's excitement about the breakthrough discovery quickly turned to concern as she realized the potential ramifications of what they had found. She knew that there were some individuals who would do anything to prevent a peaceful resolution to the conflict with the aliens, and the newfound technology could be seen as a threat by those who sought to maintain the status quo.

As she discussed the implications of the discovery with her team, they all agreed that the utmost care and discretion would be necessary. They knew that any leak of the technology could have disastrous consequences for the negotiations, and they decided to keep the discovery under wraps until they had thoroughly tested and analyzed the device.

But their precautions were not enough to prevent a major setback. A week after the discovery, the lab was hit by a major power outage. At first, the team assumed that it was just a technical glitch, but when they tried to restart the systems, they realized that the outage was due to deliberate sabotage.

Kara's heart sank as she surveyed the damage. It was clear that someone had intentionally tampered with the power grid, and the lab had suffered a major setback in its research. She knew that the timing of the sabotage was too coincidental to be a mere accident. Someone had wanted to stop their work on the alien technology, and they had succeeded in causing significant damage.

As the team worked to repair the damage and salvage what they could, Kara's mind raced with possibilities. Who could have been responsible for the sabotage? Was it someone from within the lab, or was it an external actor with an interest in the outcome of the negotiations?

As she pondered these questions, she couldn't help but feel a sense of frustration and helplessness. The delicate balance of the negotiations had already been upset by the discovery of the advanced technology, and now the sabotage had thrown their progress into even greater uncertainty. She knew that they would have to redouble their efforts to ensure that the negotiations stayed on track, but the sabotage had dealt a serious blow to their prospects.

Kara also knew that they would have to be even more vigilant in protecting the alien technology. They had to assume that there were those who would stop at nothing to prevent a successful resolution to the conflict, and the discovery of the advanced technology had put a target on their backs. The team would need to work in secret, under the radar, and with the utmost care to ensure that they could continue their research without being targeted again.

As the team worked to repair the damage, Kara couldn't help but feel a sense of unease. She knew that the sabotage was just the beginning, and that there would be more challenges and obstacles ahead. But she also knew that they had a responsibility to persevere, no matter what came their way. The stakes were too high to give up now, and she was determined to see the negotiations through to a successful conclusion, no matter what it took.

CHAPTER VI

"The Spy"

In the aftermath of the sabotage, Kara's team worked hard to repair the damage and get their research back on track. They knew that there was still a long road ahead, but they remained committed to their mission of finding a way to peacefully resolve the conflict with the aliens.

But as they worked, Kara couldn't shake the feeling that they were being watched. She noticed several times that there were people in the lab who didn't belong there, and she began to suspect that they were being spied on. It was a frightening thought, and she knew that it meant that the stakes were even higher than they had realized.

Kara didn't share her suspicions with her team, however. She knew that they had enough on their plate already, and she didn't want to cause any unnecessary panic. Instead, she decided to investigate the matter herself, and she began to keep a close eye on everyone who entered and exited the lab.

One day, Kara noticed a man in a suit who had been hanging around the entrance to the lab for a suspiciously long time. He was clearly not a scientist or researcher, and he seemed to be taking an unusual interest in their work. She decided to confront him, and she approached him with a stern look on her face.

"Can I help you?" she asked, her voice laced with suspicion.

The man smiled and held up a badge. "I'm from the government," he said. "I'm here to ensure that your work on the alien technology is in compliance with all relevant regulations and protocols."

Kara was taken aback. She knew that the government had been involved in the negotiations with the aliens, but she hadn't realized that they were monitoring their work so closely. She decided to play it cool and not give away her suspicions.

"Of course, we're more than happy to comply with any regulations or protocols," she said, trying to sound as friendly as possible. "But I must ask, why are you so interested in our work all of a sudden?"

The man shrugged. "Just doing my job," he said. "We want to make sure that everything is above board and that there are no security risks."

Kara nodded, still not entirely convinced. She knew that the man's presence was not a coincidence, and she resolved to keep an even closer eye on their work in the future.

Over the next few weeks, Kara continued to keep watch for any signs of spying or surveillance. She knew that they had to be careful and vigilant, or risk having their work derailed once again. But as the weeks went by, she began to let her guard down a bit. They had made significant progress in their research, and the negotiations with the aliens seemed to be moving in a positive direction. She allowed herself to hope that they might actually succeed in finding a peaceful solution to the conflict.

But her hopes were short-lived. One day, she arrived at the lab to find that their research had been compromised once again. It was clear that someone had broken in during the night and stolen some of their data. Kara felt her heart sink as she realized the implications of what had happened. They were now in a race against time to recover the stolen data before it fell into the wrong hands.

As she surveyed the damage, Kara knew that there was only one way to save their work and salvage the negotiations. They would have to take extreme measures to protect the rest of their data, including going off the grid and working in secret. It was a risky move, but it was the only way to keep their research safe and continue their mission to find a peaceful resolution to the conflict with the aliens.

CHAPTER VII

"The Betrayal"

Aaliyah sat in her tent, staring at the flames in her fireplace. She couldn't believe what she had just heard. Her best friend, Halima, had betrayed her. Halima was working with the enemy all along, and had been feeding them information about Aaliyah's army's movements.

Aaliyah felt a deep sense of betrayal. She and Halima had grown up together, and had always been close. Aaliyah had shared her plans and strategies with Halima, never suspecting that she was actually working against her.

She thought about the battles they had fought together, and the victories they had won. She remembered the moments of laughter and joy they had shared. And now, it was all gone. Halima had betrayed her trust, and she couldn't forgive her for that.

But Aaliyah knew she couldn't let her emotions get the better of her. She had to think rationally and come up with a plan to deal with this situation. She couldn't let Halima's betrayal destroy everything she had worked for.

Aaliyah called for her most trusted advisors and shared the news with them. They were as shocked as she was, but they quickly got to work, strategizing and planning their next move.

They decided that the best course of action was to capture Halima and interrogate her. They needed to find out how much information she had given to the enemy, and what their plans were. Aaliyah ordered her soldiers to be on the lookout for Halima, and to bring her to her tent as soon as they found her.

A few days later, Halima was captured and brought before Aaliyah. Aaliyah looked at her, feeling a mixture of anger and sadness. "How could you do this to me?" she asked, her voice barely above a whisper.

Halima looked down, unable to meet Aaliyah's eyes. "I'm sorry," she said. "I didn't mean for things to turn out this way. I was just trying to protect my family."

Aaliyah's heart softened a little. She knew how important family was to Halima. But still, what she had done was unforgivable. "You should have come to me," she said. "We could have found a way to protect your family without putting everyone else in danger."

Halima looked up, tears streaming down her face. "I know," she said. "I was foolish. Please, forgive me."

Aaliyah thought for a moment. She knew that forgiving Halima would be difficult, but she also knew that they had been friends for a long time. "I can't forgive you just yet," she said. "But I promise to take care of your family. They will be safe with us."

Halima nodded, tears still in her eyes. Aaliyah ordered her soldiers to take Halima to a safe place where her family would be taken care of. She knew that forgiving Halima would take time, but she also knew that she had to be the bigger person and do what was best for everyone.

As she watched Halima leave, Aaliyah felt a sense of relief. She had made the right decision. She knew that she couldn't let her emotions cloud her judgment, and that forgiving Halima would take time. But she was willing to try. After all, they had been friends for a long time, and she hoped that they could rebuild their friendship in time.

CHAPTER VIII

"The Mystery Deepens"

For the next few days, Alex couldn't shake off the feeling of unease. Something was off, he could sense it. But he couldn't put his finger on what it was.

He tried to focus on his work, but his mind kept wandering. He looked around the office, hoping to find something that would give him a clue. And that's when he noticed it - the security camera.

Alex had always been aware of the camera's presence, but he had never paid much attention to it. It was just another piece of equipment that he had to install and maintain. But now, he couldn't help but wonder if the camera had captured anything unusual.

He quickly logged into the security system and began going through the footage. Most of it was uneventful - just people going about their business. But then he saw something that made his heart skip a beat.

It was a figure, moving quickly across the screen. Alex couldn't make out much detail, but he knew it wasn't human. It was too large, too fast. And it was definitely not an animal.

He rewound the footage and watched it again. And again. But each time, the figure moved too quickly for him to get a clear look. He needed to find a way to slow it down, to see it in more detail.

He spent the rest of the day poring over the security system, trying to find a way to enhance the footage. But no matter what he tried, the figure remained a blur.

That night, Alex couldn't sleep. He kept thinking about the figure, wondering what it was, and what it wanted. And then he heard a sound - a faint scratching, coming from the wall.

He sat up in bed, straining to listen. The scratching grew louder, more insistent. And then, it stopped. He waited, but there was no sound.

He got out of bed and went to the wall, pressing his ear against it. And that's when he heard it - a faint whisper, too low for him to make out the words.

He pulled back, his heart racing. What was going on? Was he going crazy? Or was there really something in the walls?

He decided to investigate. He went to the basement, where the pipes and wiring were located. He searched the walls, looking for any signs of disturbance. And that's when he found it - a small hole, just big enough for something to squeeze through.

He shone his flashlight inside, but he couldn't see anything. He reached in, feeling around. And then, something grabbed his hand. He yanked it back, but it was too late. Something had latched onto his arm.

He screamed, trying to shake it off. And then, it let go, scurrying back into the darkness.

Alex stumbled back, his heart pounding. He knew he had to tell someone, but who would believe him? Who would take him seriously?

He decided to take matters into his own hands. He was going to find out what was going on, no matter what it took.

CHAPTER IX
“Revelations”

Ava woke up with a start, feeling disoriented and unsure of where she was. As her eyes adjusted to the darkness, she saw that she was in a dimly lit room, lying on a bed with a thin blanket covering her. She tried to sit up, but a sudden wave of dizziness made her lie back down.

Suddenly, a figure materialized out of the shadows. It was Adira, the leader of the Resistance. "You’re awake," Adira said with a small smile. "How are you feeling?"

Ava tried to speak, but her throat was dry. Adira handed her a glass of water, which she gratefully sipped. "Better," Ava croaked. "What happened? Where am I?"

"You’re in one of our safe houses," Adira explained. "You collapsed during the battle, so we brought you here to recuperate."

Ava tried to remember what had happened during the battle, but her memories were hazy. "Did we win?" she asked, her voice barely above a whisper.

Adira hesitated before answering. "Yes, we won," she said finally. "But at a great cost."

Ava’s heart sank. "What happened?" she asked, fearing the worst.

Adira took a deep breath. "The Echelon released a weapon that killed most of the population in the surrounding area," she said. "We were lucky to survive, but there are many casualties."

Ava felt a surge of anger and sadness. How could the Echelon be so callous with human life? "We have to stop them," she said, determination in her voice.

Adira nodded. "That's why I brought you here," she said. "There's something you need to see."

She led Ava to a room where several Resistance members were gathered around a holographic display. As Ava approached, she saw that it was a map of the city, with different colored dots representing various Echelon facilities.

"We've been monitoring their activity for some time now," Adira explained. "And we've discovered something alarming."

She pointed to a cluster of red dots on the map. "These are the main Echelon research facilities," she said. "And we've uncovered evidence that they're developing a new weapon, one that could destroy the entire city."

Ava's mind reeled at the implications. "We have to stop them," she said again, more urgently this time.

Adira nodded. "That's where you come in," she said. "You have the skills and knowledge to infiltrate their facilities and gather intel. We need to know everything we can about this weapon before it's too late."

Ava felt a surge of adrenaline. This was what she had been training for, what she had been waiting for her whole life. She was ready to do whatever it took to bring down the Echelon once and for all.

"I'm in," she said, her voice firm.

Adira smiled. "Good," she said. "We'll start planning tomorrow. For now, get some rest. You're going to need it."

As Ava lay down on the bed, her mind whirring with plans and ideas, she felt a sense of purpose and resolve that she had never felt before. She was ready to face whatever lay ahead, and to do whatever it took to ensure that the Echelon could never harm anyone again.

To be continued.

CHAPTER X

"The End"

The end had finally arrived. The experiment had failed, and the consequences were catastrophic. The people of Earth would never forget the day that the skies turned black, and the world was plunged into chaos.

The group of scientists responsible for the experiment had all died, their bodies unrecognizable after the explosion. The only survivor was Jack, who had been on the other side of the facility when it happened. He watched in horror as the world fell apart around him.

The air was thick with ash and smoke, and the ground was shaking violently. Jack stumbled through the rubble, his eyes wide with fear. He knew that he had to get out of there before it was too late.

He didn't know how long he wandered, but eventually, he came across a group of survivors. They were huddled together, staring at the destruction around them. Jack approached them cautiously, unsure if they would accept him.

To his surprise, they welcomed him with open arms. They were a small community, made up of people from all walks of life. They had all been brought together by the disaster, united in their struggle for survival.

Jack knew that he had to do whatever it took to help them. He used his knowledge of science to try and understand what had happened, but there was no explanation for the devastation that had occurred.

Despite the hopelessness of the situation, the survivors refused to give up. They worked together to gather food and water, and to build shelter from the harsh environment.

Jack did his best to help, but he couldn't shake the guilt he felt for his role in the experiment. He knew that he could never make up for the lives that had been lost.

As the days turned into weeks, the community began to adapt to their new way of life. They found joy in the simple things, like cooking a meal or telling stories around the fire.

But the world outside was still a dangerous place. There were gangs of desperate survivors, willing to do whatever it took to survive. They raided other communities for supplies, and some even resorted to cannibalism.

The community that Jack had found himself in knew that they had to defend themselves. They worked together to build a fortified wall around their encampment, using scrap metal and debris from the surrounding area.

The wall gave them a sense of safety, but it was never enough. Every night, they would take turns standing guard, watching for any signs of danger.

In the end, it was a natural disaster that would bring an end to their struggle. The skies had been dark for months, but one day, the clouds began to part. The sun shone down on the community, and they all stopped to take in the beauty of it.

But as they looked up at the sky, they saw something else. A massive asteroid was hurtling towards them, and there was nothing they could do to stop it.

The end was quick and painless. The asteroid hit with the force of a nuclear bomb, obliterating everything in its path.

And just like that, it was over. The survivors of the experiment were gone, and the world was silent once again. The only reminder of their existence was a massive crater, where their community had once stood.

In the years that followed, the crater would fill with water, becoming a lake. People would come from all over to see it, marveling at the power of nature.

But for those who had lived through the experiment, the lake would always be a reminder of the horrors they had endured. And they would never forget the lesson that they had learned the hard way: that some things should never be tampered with.

CHAPTER XI

"The Confrontation"

As soon as the group arrived at the abandoned laboratory, they were greeted by the sight of a familiar figure. It was Dr. Schmidt, the same scientist who had discovered the virus and had been responsible for its spread. He was standing at the entrance, a smug expression on his face.

"I see you've found your way here," he said, his voice dripping with sarcasm.

"What have you done?" Jessica demanded, her eyes blazing with anger.

"I've done what needed to be done," Dr. Schmidt replied calmly. "I've created the ultimate weapon, one that will bring an end to all wars and conflicts. And I've done it by harnessing the power of the virus."

The group stared at him in shock, unable to believe what they were hearing.

"You can't be serious," Michael said, his voice low and dangerous. "You've unleashed a deadly virus on the world and caused untold suffering, and now you're claiming that you've done it for the greater good?"

Dr. Schmidt just shrugged. "Sometimes sacrifices have to be made for the greater good."

"You're insane," Samantha said, her voice trembling with fury. "You don't get to play God and decide who lives and who dies."

Dr. Schmidt just smiled. "I already have."

The group tensed, ready for a fight. But Dr. Schmidt had other plans. With a wave of his hand, he activated a remote detonator, and the laboratory exploded in a shower of debris.

The group was thrown back by the force of the blast, and when they regained their senses, they saw that Dr. Schmidt was nowhere to be found.

"We have to find him," Jessica said, her voice urgent. "He can't be allowed to get away with this."

The group nodded in agreement and set off in pursuit of Dr. Schmidt. They followed his trail through the ruins of the laboratory, their determination growing with each step.

Finally, they caught up with him in a deserted alleyway. He was holding a vial of the virus in his hand, a maniacal gleam in his eye.

"Don't come any closer," he warned them. "I'll use this virus if I have to."

"You won't get away with this," Michael said, his voice steely.

"We'll stop you," Samantha added, her fists clenched.

Dr. Schmidt just laughed. "You think you can stop me? I've outsmarted all of you. I've created the ultimate weapon, and there's nothing you can do to stop me."

But the group refused to back down. They knew that they had to do whatever it took to stop Dr. Schmidt and prevent him from using the virus.

And so, they charged forward, ready for the final confrontation. The fate of the world hung in the balance, and they were determined to ensure that it was a safe and peaceful place for future generations.

CHAPTER XII

"The Ultimate Challenge"

As the day of the competition draws near, the air is thick with excitement and tension. The other teams are working just as hard as the Solar Strikers, and each one is determined to win.

Tommy, the team captain, has been feeling the pressure. He knows that his team is good, but so are the others. He can't shake the feeling that there's something they're missing, something that will give the other teams an edge.

He's been thinking about it for days, going over every detail of their training and preparation, trying to find the weak spot. And then it hits him.

"Guys, I think I know what we're missing," he says to the rest of the Solar Strikers.

"What is it?" asks Lisa.

"It's not what, it's who," says Tommy. "We need a secret weapon."

"A secret weapon?" repeats Jake. "What are you talking about?"

"We need someone who can take us to the next level," says Tommy. "Someone who's not on our team, but who can help us win."

The rest of the team looks skeptical. They've been working hard together for months, and they don't want to bring in an outsider. But Tommy is convinced that this is what they need to do.

"I have someone in mind," he says. "Someone who's an expert in strategy and tactics. Someone who can help us outthink the other teams."

"Who is it?" asks Lisa.

"Her name is Samantha," says Tommy. "She's a friend of mine from college. She's never played Solarball, but she's a genius when it comes to strategy games. I think she could really help us."

The rest of the team is still hesitant, but Tommy is persuasive. He talks to Samantha and convinces her to come to the competition and work with the Solar Strikers.

On the day of the competition, the Solar Strikers are nervous but ready. They've been practicing with Samantha for weeks, and they feel like they have a new edge. The other teams are surprised to see her with them, but they don't know what to make of it.

The Solar Strikers win their first game easily, thanks to a strategy that Samantha came up with. The second game is tougher, but they manage to pull off a win in the final minutes.

In the final game, they're up against the team that everyone thought would win. It's a hard-fought battle, with both teams playing their best. But in the end, the Solar Strikers emerge victorious, thanks to a last-minute play that Samantha came up with.

The team is elated, but they know that they couldn't have done it without Samantha. They lift her up on their shoulders and carry her off the field, cheering and celebrating their hard-won victory.

As they ride home on the bus, Tommy turns to Samantha and says, "Thanks for everything. We couldn't have done it without you."

Samantha smiles. "It was my pleasure," she says. "But I have to admit, I never thought I'd get so into a game like Solarball."

The rest of the team laughs, and they all agree that it's been an amazing experience. They've worked hard, overcome challenges, and come out on top. And they know that they'll always remember the summer that they became champions.

CHAPTER XIII

"A New Plan"

As the team settled into their new home in the underground bunker, they began to discuss their next steps. They all knew that the situation on the surface was dire, and they needed to come up with a plan to stop the alien invasion before it was too late.

Dr. Hernandez had been busy analyzing the alien technology they had recovered, and she had made some interesting discoveries. "The technology is incredibly advanced," she explained. "But it's also incredibly fragile. If we can find a way to disrupt their communication and power systems, we might be able to disable their weapons."

"That's a great idea," said Jack. "But how are we going to get close enough to do that?"

Dr. Hernandez thought for a moment. "We'll need to get inside their mothership," she said. "It's the only way to get close enough to their technology to disrupt it."

Everyone looked at each other nervously. The idea of sneaking into an alien mothership was terrifying, but they all knew it was their only option.

They spent the next few days planning their mission. They would need to use the stealth suits they had recovered to sneak onto the ship undetected. Once inside, they would split up and try to find the control room where they could disable the ship's systems.

The day of the mission arrived, and the team put on their suits and set off towards the mothership. They had studied the ship's movements and knew the best time to make their approach.

As they got closer to the ship, they could see the massive hull looming over them. They landed on a small docking platform on the side of the ship and quickly made their way inside.

The ship was a labyrinth of twisting corridors and strange, glowing machinery. They moved quickly and silently, avoiding any patrols they came across.

Finally, they found the control room. Dr. Hernandez went to work, using her knowledge of the alien technology to disable the ship's power systems. The rest of the team kept watch, making sure no one came to investigate.

As the last of the systems went down, the ship shuddered and came to a stop. They had done it.

But as they made their way back to the docking platform, they heard an alarm blaring. The aliens had discovered them, and they needed to get out of there fast.

They ran back through the twisting corridors, pursued by a swarm of alien soldiers. The team fought back, using their advanced weapons to hold off the attackers.

Finally, they burst out onto the docking platform and launched themselves back towards the surface. They could hear the aliens in pursuit, but they were no match for the team's superior technology.

As they landed back on the surface, they could see the alien ships falling from the sky, disabled by their actions. The invasion had been stopped, and the team had saved the world.

They were hailed as heroes, and their names went down in history as the people who had saved the Earth from the alien threat. But for the team, the real victory was knowing that they had come together to face a seemingly impossible challenge and had emerged victorious.

As they settled back into their normal lives, they knew that they had been changed forever by their experience. They had learned that anything was possible when they worked together and that they were capable of achieving greatness in the face of even the most daunting obstacles.

CHAPTER XIV

“The Battle”

As the sun began to rise over the mountains, the army prepared for the battle ahead. Row upon row of soldiers stood at attention, their weapons glinting in the light. Tensions were high, and everyone could feel the weight of what was to come.

Zara stood at the front of the formation, her sword at the ready. She was nervous, but she knew that she had to be brave for her soldiers. They were all looking to her for guidance and strength.

She looked around at her army, taking in the determined expressions on their faces. They had been training for this moment for months, and now it was finally here. They were ready to fight for their freedom.

Zara took a deep breath and lifted her sword high. "Today, we fight for our freedom!" she shouted, her voice ringing out over the army. "We fight for our families, our homes, and our way of life. We will not let them take it from us!"

The soldiers cheered in response, their spirits lifting at the sound of her words. Zara felt a surge of pride as she looked out over the army. She knew that they were ready.

As the sun climbed higher in the sky, the army began to march towards the enemy. Zara led the charge, her sword flashing in the light. The ground shook beneath their feet as they approached the enemy lines.

The two armies clashed with a deafening roar. Swords clashed, arrows flew, and soldiers screamed as they fell. Zara fought with all her might, her heart pounding in her chest. She could feel the heat of battle all around her, and the acrid smell of smoke filled her nostrils.

For hours, the battle raged on. The soldiers fought with everything they had, determined to win at all costs. Zara felt herself growing tired, but she knew that she couldn't give up. She had to keep fighting.

As the sun began to set, the battle finally began to turn in their favor. The enemy soldiers started to retreat, their lines breaking under the force of Zara's army. The soldiers cheered as they chased their enemies from the field.

Zara collapsed onto the ground, her sword clattering beside her. She was exhausted, but she felt a sense of satisfaction knowing that they had won. Her soldiers gathered around her, patting her on the back and thanking her for her leadership.

But even as they celebrated their victory, Zara knew that the war was far from over. They had won this battle, but there would be many more to come. She would have to stay strong and keep fighting, no matter what lay ahead.

With a deep breath, Zara stood up and sheathed her sword. She looked out over the battlefield, her eyes scanning the horizon. She knew that they had won this battle, but the war was far from over. And she was ready for whatever came next.

9 798889 861546

Printed by Libri Plureos GmbH in Hamburg, Germany